Assassination of a Homeless Man

ABDELGAFFER ELYAMANI

DEDICATION

To my parents, who feed me the notion of dignity and unconditional love. To Ms. Carole E., whom I met at Denver International Airport and sent me three books to encourage me to write my book. To Ms. Donna Zimmerman, who typed my story and organized it professionally.

Thanks to the owner William Smith, Sir Speedy, for printing, copying, graphic design, and mailing services in Denver for designing my idea in a beautiful book cover. Also, thanks to the team at CaryPress International Books for the publishing support.

Finally, my special thanks to my editor Ms. Linda Cashdan from Washington, D.C., for editing my story and encouraging me to publish; thank you for everything.

PREFACE

From my imagination to your heart, I wrote my story Assassination of a Homeless Man. It is an attempt to explore life in the 21st Century with the mind of the 21st Century to change our old school's ideas about life to cope with the 21st Century technology and a new lifestyle to enjoy short-term life on Earth.

Table of Contents

CHAPTER 1

Introduction

"Good morning, honey," said John Patrick to his wife, Jessica Johnson.

She replied with a pale smile. "Good morning, Mr. Loser."

John said, "Watch your mouth. The kids may hear you, dear. Shame on you to call their father a loser in this early morning!!!"

Jessica was sitting on the couch drinking her coffee, she put the coffee on the table and stood up. "Shame on me?" she yelled. "It is a shame on you! In a great country like this with all kind of opportunities, you're still jobless, helpless, and useless. You spend all your time with your homeless friends in Newhaven Green, with people who can't pay for their own food, eat from garbage cans, sleep in the street, and beg people for cigarettes, or money to buy alcohol!!! People from all over the world come to this country for a better life, with nothing but hope. Look at them now. They're driving brand new cars, having houses, supporting their families, paying taxes, obeying the law, developing themselves and the country. Look at their children. They go to school and colleges. They are shining like butterflies on a spring day. They started from scratch. They made it.

"But look at you. You are an accountant, but you still have nothing! That is why I have decided to kill you a week from now, if you don't have a job like everybody else!!! You know why I decided to kill you?"

"Please stop that and don't compare me with anybody," John Patrick interrupted. Because I am not anybody. I am myself. I am a man of integrity, I am an honest man and brave enough to express my own view, even if I paid a lot for that. That is huge difference.

"They put me in prison for a crime I didn't do. I lost my house. I lost my job, my money, my credit. I can't even open a bank account or vote, or even marry a woman I've spent more than fifteen years with, having two kids together."

John Patrick and Jessica Johnson had lived together as husband and wife for more than fifteen years in New Haven, Connecticut. They met the first time at the Happy

Steak House there. It was October, 1991. Since then they have been a couple. They have two kids. James is 11 and Mary is 9. Jessica was a waitress at the Happy Steak House. John Patrick was an accountant in big corporation in Newhaven.

But things changed when John Patrick was accused of fraud and locked in prison for three years. Since he got out of prison, he has refused to work again, and started hanging out with the homeless in New Haven Green. Sometimes he sleeps in the street with homeless, because Jessica is fighting with him all the time, because he doesn't want to work anymore.

"I didn't lose myself as a human being," John Patrick continued, "The system wanted me to lose my dignity after I lost my job, kiss their hands to get my job back, say sorry for something I didn't do, and be a slave to them all my life. But I will swim against the current. I will win the game, because I believe I am in the right, that it is my life, not their life. I chose to be free and not a slave to the money, I will be happy without money!!!!"

John Patrick continued. "Jessica I opened my heart to you. I gave you everything – love, money. I don't remember ever saying no to anything you asked of me, because I love you. Now you say you want to kill me because I have no money. Are you serious, just like that? Jessica, health is more important than money. When we lose our health, we lose everything. When we get sick, the first thing we do, is call off work, and go to a doctor.

"So you know Jessica, if you reach the bottom of human stupidity and arrogance, you will end you up one day in prison or hell fire. I help people in street for sake of helping, not for money. I don't take tips for that. You help people in the restaurant, but when they don't give you tips you get mad. People are broke. They don't have money. You don't understand that because you are dumb.

"Jessica, I decided to eliminate money from my life after working all my life just to make money, because I found out I could be happy without money. The homeless people found that. That is why I spend my time with them. Homeless people are very strong. They don't have jobs, they don't have a house or an apartment or any place to live, no shower, kitchen, bed or even a pillow, but they are still surviving. They don't give up on life. They still smile, in winter, in the rain, in night and day. Just like a candle in the wind, they don't give up on life, because they know the real meaning of life. A lot of people with jobs and houses and money don't know that. They kill themselves or escape through drugs and alcohol or spend their life just in vain.

"Jessica, anybody who knows the real meaning of life will never cry like you, will never get upset like you, will never kill themselves, or think of killing somebody, like what you saying to me now.

"So, Jessica, I found real life with real people in streets, I am street smart, in the fresh air. Now I am going out."

Jessica was very calm and quiet when John Patrick was speaking. As soon as he finished, she pointed a gun in his face. "I am not going to buy that, Mr. Leftover. I am going to kill you seven days from now. They only way out is to get a job. Otherwise I am going to kill you and throw your body in New Haven Green where your friends gather every day, so they can leave the place for real people, people who could face the trouble of life with courage, awareness, firmness, fearlessness and focus to find a solution, instead of sobbing, crying, begging other people for help, where they can help themselves. People who struggle and fight back, fight to the end, not for the time being, only to quit, bow down to life's stress, seek the easy way out, escaping to drugs and alcohol, begging in street for a cigarette, eating leftover food from garbage cans. Sleep in street just like that."

Jessica continued, "So, Mr. Leftover, now you know why I want to kill - to save the earth from your smell, your evil soul, your acceptance of failure, depression. Just like that without any resistance. "John Patrick, if there is a will, there is way, but you lost the will, then you lost the way." Jessica with the gun still in her hand said, "Now get out of my face, go and get a job before I change my mind and kill you now!"

John Patrick was puzzled. "Jessica, are you serious? Is this a real gun? Jessica, I know you sometimes smoked weed-"

"I smoked sometimes," she interrupted, but I am not addicted like you. Mind your business. Get out of my face now!"

John Patrick left his transitional house in Fairhaven in very bad shape, shivering, shaking, although it was summer. He was talking to himself loudly, when he reached the New Haven Green where homeless people gathered in the morning every day, The distance from his house in Fairhaven was just five miles. The homeless in the area, when they looked at him, rushed to him asking, "What happened to you?" because he was a very kind man, always making jokes, trying all the time to help everyone and listen to their problems.

Jack Nelson was the first one who came close and asked him, "Please tell me what happened? Don't panic. We all here for you." Jack Nelson had been a famous criminal lawyer, but he lost his job for malpractice, and after being locked up in prison for ten years, he became homeless. The homeless people called him "the president of the Green." He was a very close friend to John Patrick.

"Jessica, my wife, she wants to kill me," John Patrick said, "She put a gun in my face this morning. It was a real gun."

"Why she want to kill you? Jack Nelson asked, laughing "You're almost a dead man already." "She wants me to get a job."

Jack Nelson laughed again. "Man, that is very easy. I thought something big happened to you."

John was still shaking. "I lived with Jessica more than fifteen years. I have never seen her like today. She pointed a gun in my face. She forgot the love, our peaceful life together. She forgot our kids. She forget everything. Just like that!"

Jack Nelson gave him a hug. "Listen to me, my friend. First, don't panic. Second, about the job, that is very easy. I know a friend of mine who works with fake ID's. He can give you a fake pay stub as if you have a job, so you can tell her, 'I got a job as a cashier. That is easy. Because of your history, she knows you can get a job that easily, so you don't have to kill yourself. Life is short. Forget this incident. Let it go. We need you here in the Green. Everybody loves you."

They all gave him a hug. Eventually John Patrick felt comforted and his smile was again shining on his face like the man he used to be, making jokes, listening patiently to his friends, solving their daily problems!!!

But in the afternoon, while all the homeless were chatting in New Haven Green and laughing as if they were sitting in a red carpet club, something terrible happened. Jessica came to the Green, John Patrick's favorite spot, and in front of everybody said, "You're still here? I was not playing. I am going to kill you a week from now, as I promised. You better be ready for the hellfire." And very soon she left the Green. Everybody heard what she said. Everybody was mad, but nobody said anything, even John Patrick himself.

Jack Nelson came to John Patrick and said, "My friend, to be honest with you, in the morning when you told me your story, I didn't believe you, but now after what happened in front of me, I am telling you: don't go to your wife's house. You'd better not come to New Haven Green or, better yet, leave Connecticut. I saw the evil in her eyes and heard the determination in her voice. She meant what she said. That is something serious. I have an uncle who lives in New Mexico. He is a good man. He has a chicken farm in Santa Fe. You can go and work with him for now. I have his phone number. I can call him now. I am going to tell him about you. He is a good man. Take whatever money he gives you and you can stay on the farm. They provide housing and free food for the workers. I feel, as a criminal lawyer, something terrible may happen very soon to you, if you stay here. This is a matter of life and death. So, think about it and tell me what you are going to do about this. Very soon, my friend, very soon."

CHAPTER 2

John Patrick Life Lessons

John Patrick stood up in front of his homeless friends and said, "My friends, don't think I was afraid, maybe for time being. But I believe the human being is only creature on the earth who can adapt himself to any environmental change and win. So, my friends, we can't force a human being to do things he doesn't like or wash a human being's brain with fake ideas. When this happens to the human being, that will be the weakest moment in human history on Earth. Finally the human being will rise up against this weakness and win the honor of being a human being again!!! Life is not about having a job or not having a job. It is not about having money or not having money. Life is not about having money in a bank or having a bank itself!

"Life is about morals first and last. When we don't have morals, we don't have life. That is why they call us human beings. So we have to respect human values, share these values with everybody around us - parents, kids, family, friends, neighbors, even the animal who live with us - so we can better our lives every day the sun comes out and declares a new day, sharing our leftover food, furniture, anything we don't want, to those who don't have it, even leftover money. Then, we can taste the nectar of life, deserve the honor of being human beings on this amazing earth. Discover the beauty in the world, the beauty inside us, build more values, for us and to generations to come! So my friends, life is very simple but sick ideas in our minds can misinterpret life and make our lives miserable and stressful. What do people do when they go to parks? They throw away their leftover food. Even restaurants and grocery stores at the end of the day throw food away in trash cans.

"So the homeless, including me, take care of that leftover, eat the leftover food, recycle the cans, bottles. We, the homeless people, are the witnesses in the court of life that leftover food alone can solve the problem of poverty in this country, maybe in the whole world. That is why my wife called me Mr. Leftover, but who cares? The leftovers alone make our lives roll along, leaving , the rest for fun, families, friends. Working two jobs or sometimes three jobs, working long hours is crazy, and is homicide to our lives, kids, health, mentally, physically. When are we going to see our children, wives, husbands, if we leave the house at 6 a.m. and come back at 10 p.m.? What kind of life is that? Even if we get money, we don't have time to spend it, if we work 7 days a week. That is why the enemy of fun says life start at 60 and at 50. They start selling funeral plans, even before you finish your home mortgage! That is insane!

"When I became homeless, I believe strongly my life started at day one. We must enjoy our lives from day one to the end, because life is very short. Some people are born dead, some people die at day one or two, but even if you live up to 100, life still goes very fast, and fades away like a dream.

"So my friends, who put this idea in our minds, that we should work all our lives to enjoy life when we reach 60. We have to be creative. Life could be end at any moment with warning or without warning with reason or without reason, so we have to be creative and use life to the fullest. Enjoy every moment. That's why I believe retirement should be at 50, called "creative retirement," where we can still enjoy our lives while we are in good shape., because retirement means we have to save money for when we can't work anymore. But I believe we have to have money, health, and a good time to live life, feel alive. I guess 50 years is enough time to start a new life, free from hassles and not repeat the first 50 years and not repeat the same stupid mistakes."

John Patrick continued, "Let me tell you the story of a businessman who decided to be a millionaire. He worked very hard, left the house at 5 a.m. and came back at 10 p.m. for seven days a week. He made good money. But what happened was his wife called him one day to come home to bury his four-year-old son, When he came home, his wife gave him the car keys and house keys. She told him 'It was a big mistake I made in my life. I married you,' and she left everything to go her own way.

"The businessman was depressed and started crying every day. The doctor told him 'Death is very natural. It happens just like that. You don't have to be old to die or young or healthy or sick. Death is the end for human beings on earth. Even all creatures, animals and plants have life spans.

"The businessman said to the doctor, 'I know that doctor, but I cry and feel depressed, because when my son was born, I was on a business trip. All his four years I left the house early in the morning, while my son was asleep and came home late while he slept too. I never took him to a park or spent a weekend with him for four years. When I sometimes came home, he was in daycare. I never listened to my wife when she said to me, 'Your family is more important than money,' but now I realize that my family was more important than money. I lost my son and my wife too. She will never forgive me, but it is too late.' "

John Patrick continued, "My friends, I am going to tell you what happened to Mrs. Cartwright when she passed away in New Haven Green last year.

"Mrs. Cartwright, an elderly homeless woman, lived in New Haven between the shelter and the street. She was a very nice lady. I know all of you know her. She was a mother of two kids. She raised them. One is a doctor and the other is a teacher. But Mrs. Cartwright was rich, lived in a suburb of San Francisco, California. When her husband died, her two sons decided to take her property and money account, by claiming she was a dementia patient and couldn't take care of herself and property. They put her in a nursing home. But Mrs. Cartwright escaped from the nursing home, left all California, to come to the east coast and become a homeless in New Haven, Connecticut.

"But the sad part was, when her sons put her in the nursing home, they told the nursing home management that if their mother passed away in the nursing home, they should burn her body and send them her ashes in the mail!!!

"Mrs. Cartwright knew about that, but she don't go to court after her two sons. But when she died in New Haven Green last year, they found in her purse a letter.

"I am going to tell you what she said in her letter. I kept the letter in my mind. I will never in my life forget it. Mrs. Cartwright said in her letter:

I am Barbara Cartwright. Please don't burn my body, because this body has a beautiful heart inside, who loved a beautiful husband, Mr. Cartwright, for 50 years. I never cheated on him, raised two kids, one was a doctor, the second, a teacher. I gave them everything, but they both changed when they got married. I still love them. Don't burn my body. Put my body in the earth. Let my body melt with the earth, because I love the earth where I walked all my life to do good things for myself and my family, and my community. I never walked on the earth to harm anybody, I am not perfect but I am a beautiful person. With money we can make life better, without money still we can enjoy life, and make others happy too. Please don't burn my body.

"So my friends, when we think too much about money, we will become like the businessman who forget his son for four years, till he died, or become like Mrs. Cartwright's sons who put her in nursing home, waiting her to die and send them her ashes in mail."

John Patrick continued, "I want to tell you why I brought my kids to the Green. Jessica was not happy, but I have a point. I brought my kids because I want teach them the real life, how the police officers arrest in streets the criminal. The police force are not our enemies. The criminals are our enemies. Can you imagine if there were no police for one day or even for one hour? The criminals want to steal our smiles and money and property to buy a drugs or alcohol. The police want stop them and make us safe.

"So I teach my kids to respect the law, and report anything to law enforcement. That is the only way to be safe, otherwise you will be in prison. I brought my kids to see in the streets, the diversity, different people and different colors, different races, that this is part of the nature of life. Diversity in the animal kingdom and plant, even in rocks and water - there is fresh water and salt water.

"I teach them in human life not to look to people's color or races, but to pay attention only to human behavior. That is the only way to know people. Make friends with people and love them and respect them, because that behavior tells people what is inside us.

"I teach them to look in streets how everybody is unique, because everybody has a fingerprint different from everybody else in the whole world, even their parents. So when somebody makes mistake, look to him as individual (not their family or anybody else) because he or she is responsible for what was done.

"I teach my kids when I brought them in street to thank anybody who does anything to them, even smile. I teach them the effect of smiling in people face, the effect of good words, just like 'Are you okay? Can I help you?' because in street you find some people just want somebody to smile in their face or even say, 'How are you?' You can say to somebody with a dog, 'Your dog is beautiful' and then the conversation starts. It is hard to find it in school books. By the way, my friends, why are kids killed in schools!? School should be the safest places in the earth, because it is the place where we get knowledge, science.

"Our children need love and care, they don't need condemnation. They need a chance to express themselves in very peaceful way. They need to understand the teenage years are a stage where human beings move from childhood to adulthood with help from their parents and school. Everything will be all right with little patience and courage. We can pass this stage successfully with no pain or sorrows. Otherwise we are going to have 12 \13 year old girls with babies without fathers, with mentally sick single men in this very young age. Our children need real care, real hugs, real love. They are our future family leaders. We should take them very seriously. Stop playing with their future, their lives. We need them; they need us. That why I brought my kids to show them this real life in real streets to become street smart, cope with real life matters.

"So my friends, I am going to tell you the story of my 9 year-old daughter, when she saw a little girl in New Haven Green pushing a stroller with her one-year-old daughter.

"So my daughter, when she saw a little girl pushing the stroller, she asked the girl, 'Is that your baby sister?' The little girl said, 'No it is my daughter.' My daughter asked, 'How old are you and how old is your daughter?' the little girl said, 'I am fourteen, my daughter is one year old.' My daughter said, 'Where is the father of your daughter?' The little girl cried and said, 'I don't know, I am a foster kid. I live with a foster mom. I don't even know my mom or my own dad.'

"My daughter hugged the little girl and said, 'I wish you and your daughter a happy life.' She gave her a piece of candy. She came and told me the story, and said to me, 'I will never get pregnant till I get married. I don't want to be in the situation of that little girl. That is not fun. It is very sad.' She wrote something like a poem. I am going to say it to you. My daughter said in her poem:

I saw two little girls in New Haven Green
The little one in stroller
The big one pushing the stroller
The little one is one year old and is a daughter
The big one is fourteen years old and is a mother
The little one doesn't talk
The big little one talks
She talks about missing parents
She talks about missing hugs
She talks about missing Grandma
She talks about missing Grandpa
She talks about missing people to trust, missing true
    friends
She talks about her abusing first foster mom, who
    smiles at her only when she get her paycheck
She talks about her abusing second foster mom who
    never smiles at her

She talks about her third foster mom who is acting nice, but she is not

She talks about the dog who followed the scent to search for her mom

She talks about the dog returning who said I found the lady who hugged you when you came out

She is a nurse, because your smell still in her, your real mom, disappeared, after you come out!!!

Finally she talked about the missing father of her daughter!!!

John Patrick continued, "My son too, gets 'A+' in street class with me. When he saw two teenager gangs fighting in street, and one teen get killed, the thing that made my son happy was the arrival of the police who broke up the fight. Otherwise a lot of teens would be killed.

"My son told me, 'I will never, ever join any gang in my life. When I grow up I want to be a police officer, so I can help people to be safe and happy.' My son uses his own sense to make this decisions, uses his own eyes, feelings and mind, at the spot. That is why I gave him A+. That is my point. That is why bring my kids to the streets!!!"

John Patrick continued, "I am sorry my friends I took long time express my feelings to you, but I want to show you I am not a coward, but I want say something very important. That when I was an accountant in a big company, I had a lot of money in my account, a house, cars. I have a brother who has seven children, works three jobs to take care of his family. I never helped him, even with gift cards to his family, but when I was in prison, he was the only one who visited me every month and put some money for my commissary in prison. I learned the most important thing in life is your family. I learned what is the meaning of brotherhood. That is more important than money, That is real credit, a real backup in life. I am glad I know that. I will promise, I will be new person. I am sure it is not too late for me.

"So please my friends, tell Jessica to leave me alone." He started crying like a baby. All the homeless, who listened to him comforted him!!!

CHAPTER 3

David's Letter

John Patrick went back to his favorite spot. David came to John Patrick with a letter in his hand said, "Please, wise man, read this letter. It is from my parents in Africa. I received it through one of my native country friends. Tell me what to do because I'm fed up. I feel I am going to die."

David was an African immigrant who come to United States 20 years ago for a better life and end up drug trafficking, was locked in prison for ten years, and now is homeless. His American wife took the custody of his two kids. He is fighting for citizenship and against possible deportation because of his felony, but for now he was homeless in New Haven. John Patrick always helped him. He considered John Patrick his best friend.

John Patrick looked at him. "David, did you eat anything today?"

David said, "I am not hungry. I feel depressed. I didn't know what I was going to do after I read my parents letter. Please read the letter. Tell me what to do."

John Patrick open the letter.

Our beloved son David,

How are you? We miss you. What happened ? It is 20 years since you left your beloved village. Everybody says America is great country, that everybody there is rich, happy, and free to do what he wants to do. It is like lost paradise for all people in the world. When people go to America, and come back to their homes, they build big houses and make big businesses and live like kings. But, our son, what is wrong with you? What happened to you? When you will come back home? We become old now. The time is going fast. If we live today, we are not guaranteed to live for tomorrow. Why are you still fighting for citizenship? What are you going to do with citizenship if you lose yourself. You are already a citizen back home here in Africa.

Our son, our village now is growing up. There are schools, hospitals, even colleges. You remember that when you were little you used to run on the farm playing with animals helps to get us the milk from the goats. Our son, we still love you. Everybody in the village still remembers you, loves you, always asks about you.

Our Son, if you fail to make it in America, that is not the end of the world. Come back home. Your grandfather saw in his sleep very big dream. He insisted we tell you about his dream. Your grandfather said, "I saw in my dream, all young Africans fleeing their countries, running from war and poverty in Africa to anywhere but not Africa, young Africans running in bare feet on deserts and in boats on seas and oceans without any travel documents.

"They heard a loud, clear voice saying, "Stop, young people. Come back to your land, to your houses and parents." The young people heard the voice clearly and said, "Who are you?"

The voice said, "I am a wise man of Kilimanjaro Mount. I see all Africa from this peak. Africa is big and beautiful. In Africa you have everything. You have your parents and our history. You have rivers and mountains. You have all kinds of food, fruits, vegetables, animals, and gold and oil and diamonds and more. Don't go elsewhere. Come back now!!!"

The young people said, "In the land there are snakes and scorpions. They make our life miserable.

We escape because we can't get rid of them. We are running for our lives."

The wise man said, "The snakes and scorpions are man- made. They are fake. Please listen to me. Just come back running towards them without fear because the fear is the factor. It makes you scared and makes them bigger. They will disappear for good.

"Trust me, young people. They will run away and disappear for good, because what you are doing now is like committing suicide. You throw yourselves in deserts and oceans without travel documentation. Just like that, to unknown places, to unknown people. You are very young. You shouldn't give up easily!"

The young Africans listened to the Mt Kilimanjaro wise man. They came back to their land and without fear, they ran toward the snakes and scorpions. As soon as the snakes and scorpions saw the young people running towards them without fear, they just disappeared for good. The young people were happy. They said, "The wise man was right."

Then they started working on their land. They got fresh foods, fruits and vegetables. They took care of their animals. They ate fresh meat, drank fresh milk. From the skin of their animals, they make beautiful shoes. They danced, the dance of the victory. The dug one more time in their land, They get the gold and oil and diamonds, and they wrote a new description of Africa.

A for After, F for Fantastic, R for Revaluation, I for I am, C for Coming, A for Again it become. After this fantastic reevaluation, instead of running from Africa, and leaving it to snakes and scorpions, they built it anew.

The young Africans light candles and march to the wise man of Mt. Kilimanjaro for his advice, but again the wise man of Kilimanjaro said, "Please, we don't need the light of the candles, because the light is in you. Pass it on, and go back to work and open the doors of Africa to freedom lovers from all over the world."

The young Africans went back to work and opened the doors of Africa to freedom lovers from all over the world. That is the end of your grandfather's dream!!

So, our son, please come back home. We want you to enjoy your the life you left, because life is short. Please pack your stuff and come back. Don't miss the golden opportunity. We are still alive. We still love *you. Everybody in the village still remembers you, and loves you too. Please hurry up.*

Your beloved parents.

After he read the letter of David's parents, John Patrick whispered to himself, "David is homeless in America, fighting for citizenship to stay by his kids. He has no family member to support him. He has no money. That is very sad. But I am homeless too. My wife wants to kill me. I wish I could help him."

David was still waiting to get answer from John Patrick, so finally John Patrick said, "David, my friend, not today. My wife wants to kill me. She pulled a gun on me this morning. Please come tomorrow. I will tell you what to do."

David left him with eyes full of tears.

CHAPTER 4

Jack Nelson

After David left, John Patrick went to Jack Nelson's favorite spot. All the homeless in New Haven Green have a favorite spot, Most of the time it is on the edges and the corners of New Haven Green far from the middle areas so they can get a little privacy for themselves or imagine they have a kind of privacy.

He found Jack Nelson sitting on the grass, smoking a cigarette and asked him,. "Where have my life and family dreams gone, my friend?"

Jack Nelson said, "Your dreams faded away when you entered the prison. You will have a record that will go with you to your grave. Remember that you must pay money before they put your body in that grave. Does that make sense? I forget the name, but in one of the poorest country in the world when people die, all the funeral expenses and the land where they bury the body is free, because the only ones who pay taxes are living beings, It is a moral law. We shouldn't charge the dead people, it should be a community job, so every living human being takes part in that job. People volunteer to do this job with open hearts! So that should be your dream, die free and laugh."

Jack Nelson continued. "Your dream faded away when you lost your house and job, lost your credit and now everybody in country, maybe in the whole world, knows you have a bad credit and a criminal record. You lost your dream when you lost your freedom, had to have a parole officer running after you, even after you did your time in prison and you're under probation time. There is a question in any job application, 'Did you do time?' You know I was a criminal lawyer. I believe they should eliminate this question from job applications, because nobody is perfect. Everybody can change, for a reason or for no reason from a good person to a bad person. When somebody commits a crime, yes, he or she should go to prison and do their time, but after they do their time, they should set them free, just like that. So they can feel alive again and start a new life, because they know what the meaning of freedom is and they know their mistakes, and they paid for their mistakes. Their records should be in the courts or police force, but nobody else should know about that unless it is a special crime. The public should know about it. Other than that, let the inmates start new lives after they do the time. You get more confidence without probation or parole officer. Then the number of jobless people would decrease, the number of homeless would decrease, the number of crimes would decrease, the number of employees would increase, and everybody would feel safe and happy, again!!! Because life is simple. You're born and live and die. If they did a crime again, then they would go to prison, again and again, just like that. We must forgive each other when we hurt each other. At the same time, we should pay for our mistakes, because forgiveness is the only way to make us live a better life.

"But if we keep tracking people in their private lives to catch their mistakes, we steal their dreams, their smiles, their lives, that is why there is homelessness. That is why people go back again to prison to remain unknown, die unknown."

Jack Nelson continued, "My friend is that a dream - to build a house in this earth that's full of land? To work almost 30 years of your life to pay for your dream home, where everybody can have a free piece of land to build a house, free piece of land to be buried in, a free piece of land to make a farm and enjoy nature. And still the earth is big even still there are millions of acres of land untouched yet by man. This basic human need, just like water and oxygen, should be free. You shouldn't need 30 years of work to gain it, die, and leave it. That makes no sense at all. In life we need a place to live and a place to die, just like that. That is not a dream. A dream, my friend, is to build a house on the moon or on Mars or living in another planet where the rules will be different from the earth rules, where there is no gravity, where the day is different from our day, a place where human health is not a business, not something we see every day and act like we don't see, something called foreclosure. Foreclosure means they take your dream home, and let the rats and cats, and bugs, live in it for free, Then the poor human being becomes homeless, his dream home occupied for free by the animal kingdom members."

Jack Nelson continued, "You know, my friend besides being a lawyer I am a cartoonist. Whenever I come across a sign of a house 'foreclosure,' I stop to look inside the house. I can see rats, cats, insects. I can imagine that they are talking to each other, and the animals say,, 'We are glad we are not human beings. Do you guys remember, when those houses were occupied by human beings, they were clean and beautiful, and smelled good. Now they kick out the human beings, let them become homeless in streets and let us stay here for free for months, maybe years. That makes no sense. Even the earth is real big, we guess, all human being should go to mental hospital, because this has nothing to do with money. This is a mental health issue and is very serious, They need professional psychiatrists to fix it now!' "

Jack Nelson continued. "So, my friend, we are here in streets having fun, while other people struggle to pay their dream home, but all of us are going to die and leave not only the dream home, but the earth itself and leave everything. But we are happy. I don't know if the ones who have the dream home are happy. Life is short. Don't worry about the dream. Just stay out of trouble. Don't go to your wife, Jessica, Try all the time to enjoy every moment of your life because it could be the last moment in your life. So live it with dignity, respect and honest and be brave all the time and never give up."

Jack Nelson left John Patrick saying, "I have to go now. I will see you later my friend."

John Patrick said to him, "Now I know why they called you 'the president of the Green.'"

CHAPTER 5

Martin Franklin

A round 10 p.m. John Patrick went back again to his favorite spot in New Haven Green, sitting alone. It was dark. The light in New Haven Green was not bright, but still people moved easily in and out. John Patrick started talking to himself, not too loud but loud enough for anyone nearby him hear what he said. "I am 55 years old. I love my country, I love my family, but my wife wants to kill me because I don't have the money I had before. It is not about a job. It is about the money. She is weak. She is not honest. She doesn't say, 'I want money.' She loves the money. She doesn't love me!

"I looked into her eyes when she pulled the gun on me this morning, searching for love and the good memories of the good times we had together, of our kids, of everything I gave to her. I couldn't find anything of all that. I just saw an evil person, a different person full of hate, prejudice. I saw a criminal face. I didn't see my sweet Jessica." He started crying again like a baby.

But suddenly, he heard a voice say, "Stop crying. She doesn't deserve those tears. You are a good man. You are the most beautiful person I have ever met in my life."

John Patrick stood up and said, "Who is that?"

The voice said, "I am Martin Franklin. Did you forget about me?"

John Patrick smiled and hugged him. "Hi Martin. Long time no see. I've missed you, but Martin I cry because I lost my love for Jessica. She wanted to kill me. This morning she pulled a gun on my face. After all this years, you know Martin."

Martin Franklin had been homeless for a while. He had a felony too. He met John Patrick in New Haven Green. John Patrick considered him as a good friend. When Martin got a job at a dollar store in the New Haven Mall, he always helped John Patrick - buy him a lunch or give him a few dollars. He knew John Patrick's story, how he get into prison his family, kids.

Martin Franklin said, "I came to this place because I know you were going to be here. I know this is your favorite place. I met Jack Nelson. He told me your story. It is sad but you should be strong to get past this stage. It can happen in any family in the world. It is part of being human being, to make mistakes. Some mistakes are stupid, but that's the way it is, my friend. Get up. Stop crying, I know you can do it. Forget Jessica. That was her choice. She is crazy, but that's her choice. Now find a way to get your children from her. She might think of killing the kids too. Please my friend, close this chapter of your life. Start a new life. I know you can do it. I believe you are a very good person inside, never give up."

John Patrick said, "Thank you, Martin, I really need this encouragement now. I really appreciate it."

John Patrick added, "By the way Martin, where do you work now? I saw the dollar store in the mall closed. What happened?"

Martin said, "The owner of the store went back to his home country, Indonesia. Now I work a temp job with Labor Ready in New Haven till I can get a good job. You know I had a felony too. I don't want to be a dishwasher."

John Patrick said, "Do you know, Indonesia is largest Muslim country in world with a population like 300 million?"

Martin Franklin said, "Yes, I know. The owner of store is Muslim. I worked with him for two years He told me why Muslims pray five times a day. It is very interesting story. He said it has to do with five phenomena that happen during the day - dawn, noon, afternoon, sunset, night. So the Muslims pray at those specific times to remember Allah who made those phenomena, because nobody can do that except the creator who is Allah. Muslim believe Allah is the creator. He is one. They worship him alone, just like that."

John Patrick said, "Thank you for this information. It is first time in my life I realized why Muslims pray five times a day."

Martin Franklin said, "They still can pray any time they want, but the five times are a must and are for life because those five changes in a day happen every day!"

He continued, "I wish I could stay with you long time. I feel you are upset my friend, but as I said I have no job. I want some money, so I want to go to Labor Ready tomorrow to get a job. You know I have to be up early in the morning. Labor Ready is company which hires people without background checks, and gives the money at the end of shift. Is temporary job every day. Sometimes it lasts for a few days. Some who work there are homeless and in between jobs making some money."

Martin Franklin left John Patrick, putting some money in his hand as he usually did, giving him a good hug. "Never give up my friend."

CHAPTER 6

Tanita William

It was almost 11 p.m. when Martin Franklin left his friend, John Patrick, alone in New Haven Green. John Patrick again started whispering to himself. "Martin is right. I shouldn't go back to Jessica. I should forget about her forever. She wants to take my life. I am going to start a new life. I am not going to give up. Yes, I remember I read a beautiful article in newspaper. It was about an amazing professor named Tanita William. She had a brilliant idea about how to start a new life. She established something called "I Am Women." Those groups of women believe marriage is safe way of sex, that sex without marriage is just like a carriage without a horse, that you end up with babies without father - or mother too, because both parents may run away and leave the child alone!

Tanita William the leader of this group, is a physician, a psychiatrist. She decided not to have sex till she get married. She succeeded and that's why she found this group. Her story is a very interesting one. She said in the newspaper article, "I looked at my family history. I couldn't find the word marriage. My mom met my dad in a nightclub in the Washington, D.C. area. She spent a night with him in a motel, and in the morning my dad got arrested because he was a drug dealer. When my mom went to visit him in jail, she found out he had a different name. Her dad died in prison due to gang violence. Her mom ended up in St. Elizabeth Mental Hospital in Washington, D.C.."

Professor Tanita William wrote, "My grandmother was a stripper, but she quit her job. She went back to school again and became a nurse. She was the one who took care of me. She taught me to be strong and brave. I remember she use to tell me "You can be a cheerleader, but be a true leader. That is a way you can make difference in your life, and the lives of the other people around you." My grandmother said to me, "Sexual desire is natural in all human beings, men and women, but it is a self-control issue. Don't listen when weak people say, I can't control myself, or I can't resist the temptation inside me. As human beings we have a power to control ourselves, the brave people know that power, they are always safe and happy!!!"

So Tanita William's grandmother continued, "My beloved child, when you grow up and find a man who wants to have a relationship with you, the first question to ask him is, 'why me?' because with this question you put him in position to tell the truth or to lie? Because whatever he says will soon come out. The second statement you need to make is, 'no sex in our relationship till we talk and know each other.' And then you must say, 'now you know me and I know you. I don't want to have sex with you, but I do want to marry you. Do you want to marry me?' If he says 'Yes,' bring this man to my house. I will make you the best wedding in the earth!! If he says 'No marriage,' just tell him, 'I am a natural woman looking for natural man.' Close the chapter right away. Never ever talk to him again or meet him again because he is not the right man. If you keep doing this you will find the right man who knows you, wants you, wants to respect you, and wants to marry you! Just be very patient, strong, and never ever let anyone steal your smile and remember life is short, and can fade away like a dream. Don't spend it with a stupid person who just wants to have sex with you whenever he wants and leave you whenever he wants without any respect or responsibility, as if you are a sex machine, not a human being."

Tanita William's grandmother continued, "But my sweetheart, if you decide to get a tattoo, go to a party with the wrong crowd and end up pregnant, and come to tell me you are sorry, I will not let you down, because you are my baby girl. But I will ask you the same question I asked your mom, 'Who is a father of your child, because having a baby without a father is not fun!' The child is not a toy but a human being. When he or she grows up he or she will ask you the same question, 'Where is my dad?' You must be ready to tell the truth. A child needs a dad to hug him, raise him, and dance with him, not pay for his support every month and run away!

"My dearest baby, in life you are going to see a lot of things, both ugly and beautiful. You must always choose between them, whatever your choose that will be your choice and you will have to live with it.

"But still I will be there for you, whatever kind of life you choose. I will be there for you. I promise I will never let you down, because I love you from the bottom of my heart. But promise me too. Don't let me down."

Tanita William said, "Listen carefully to what Grandma said to me. I promised her I would never let her down. I fulfilled my promise. I never had sex till I got married. I found the right man. I went to medical school. I had three children. I finished my PhD. I am a professor. I chose the life I wanted. I went through a lot of things in my life, but I always remembered my grandma's advice: 'In life you find both the ugly and the beautiful' and I always chose the beautiful and ignored the ugly stuff."

Tanita William Programs

Tanita William has a vision and a sunny outlook on life and family in the 21st Century.

She said, "Technology in the 21st Century will become like pollen to the flowers bringing new ideas and new tools and even new jobs. It will increase our sense of freedom of choice and make life easier and simpler and shorten the distance between countries that will make life safer and bring more happiness and joy to human life."

It Happens Now

So Tanita William created special programs for everyone from women and children to adults and the elderly to prison inmates. She started testing those programs to see the impact on real life. The first program for women was called "It Happens Now." This program was to report any abuse against women like sexual harassment or rape, because the delay in reporting those kinds of things has an effect on the lives of women and their families in the future, and even on all of society, because otherwise we leave those criminals free to repeat the same things.

She suggest a new idea called "Forehead Chip" for women to wear it in their foreheads, a very delicate chip that could take the picture of anyone who tries to assault a woman right away. This chip would be connected with social media and GPS to know the location so that anybody can help and call "911." This idea would help women to report a crime on the spot, and catch the criminal right away without fear and sorrow in the future.

Foster After Talk and Walk

The second program was called "Foster After Talk and Walk," a program for children. Tanita William said, "This is a love program, because when women have a baby, whether the woman is a teenager or an adult, when they have not planned for that baby, the first thing they will think of is to get rid of that child, by giving the child to a foster mom or a family to adopt or just leave it in the hospital or somewhere and run away."

Professor William said, "That is very sad and painful. That is why I created this program to convince women to keep their children. A child is not a toy to get rid of. It is your child and you are the mother of that child" Professor Tanita said, "I imagine if the little child could talk when he or she came out, he or she would say 'You are who brought me to life and I am very young to take care of myself. I am just a few hours old. Shame on you, leaving me alone in this early stage, and shame on you to think of getting rid of me. You are my biological mother. You are my legal mother. If I had any power now, I would take you to court to take care of me. I am very sure I would win the case because I'd have a strong case. I can't take care of myself at this age! Nobody else in the whole world has anything to do with my presence in life. It is only you, you alone!!! Don't cry, take care of me. I will promise I will take care of you when I will grow up. I love you because I am a part of you and I don't want to go to anybody but you, because you are my mother. I am yours. I am proud of you!"

So Tanita William tries to tell mothers, "If you are not ready to have a child, there is nothing wrong with that. It could be very easy to fix it. Just wait for the child to talk and walk, then, you can give the child to somebody who will ready to adopt the child." Meanwhile the program will support the mother with food and place to live, medical help and even a job. Just till the child can walk and talk. Then you finish the program and you are free to do what you feel will be safe and secure for the child. Professor Tanita William with this program wants to support women in this critical situation and show them that getting rid of their own child is not an easy decision. It is a point. It will shape the character of a human being. This human being is part of society. When you take care of that human being you build built a better society and whole world!

Tanita William says, "90% of the women in the program kept their children with them after they seeing them walk and talk. Saying 'Mom'." She cited an example, Ms. Jasmine who her first child after her boyfriend ran away when he found out she was pregnant. When she gave birth to her first child, Jasmine's mother went to her boyfriend to tell him he had a son, and he had to give him his last name. Jasmine's boyfriend refused, saying, "He is not my son. I am not going to give him my last name!"

Jasmine said, "I had only one boyfriend in my life. He was my sweet heart. He took my virginity. I thought he was like that, but when I got pregnant, and had my first child, I knew he was not. I was about to kill myself, but I didn't. The program helped me to see myself. I am strong now. The turning point in my life was when my son talked to me, and said, 'Mom'. That's when I felt I was a great person. I went back to school. I finished my high school diploma. I am at college now. I got a scholarship. I am going to be a doctor. I am going to be a psychiatrist, like Professor Tanita William. I am very happy person. I have my own place now. I live close to my mom's house. I started building my own library. I became a different person. My son gave me my life back. I am glad I kept him with me!"

Jasmine continued, "I got a DNA test for my son. The result was that my boyfriend was father of my son. I knew that before, but this is now a legal process. So I took my son to my boyfriend at his work. He works as a dishwasher in a downtown restaurant. When he saw me he thought I wanted to come back to him. He want give me a hug. I refused."

I said, "This is the DNA result. This is your son." My son was with me and he could talk. I said to my son, "This your dad." He said, "Hi, dad." My boyfriend was puzzled.

Before he said anything I said, "I brought him to you to tell him that he has a dad, a dad who ran away when I was pregnant, a dad who refused to give you his last name. I'm here to show you the result. He is legally your son, but I am going to take care of him, because I heard you have a few children with some poor women. You don't even know where they are now. But I am a different person now. I am in college. I have my own car, my own place. I am going to be a psychiatrist to treat people like you, to help women to be strong and brave. You think I am going to kill myself or become drug addict. No, I am strong. I am a mother who loves her child. I am not going to be stupid again and hug anyone who offers me a hug. I am going to wait for my right man, not you."

I left my boyfriend, drove my son to my mom's house, because I had an evening class. I was happy again.

Tanita William convinced a million women worldwide to keep their children with them. They called Professor Tanita "A mom of the million."

Pulling Not Bullying

The third program was for schools and was called, "Pulling Not Bullying." The program was designed because schools were not safe anymore. "Every other day kids were getting killed in schools. She said, "The best way to stop this mess is by pulling out the bad kids before they do anything stupid and harm themselves or harm the other kids and teachers and their families, the whole society." She continued, in real life the police in streets, pull over some cars on the road. Not every car, but the ones who do something illegal or suspicious or something crazy on the road. It is the same idea. In school we see some kids doing some things crazy, bullying, but we don't do anything. We just wait till they kill somebody. That not going to solve the problem."

Professor Tanita said, "We must train teachers and students, anyone who works in the school environment including school bus drivers, school office employees, and parents to report any students' misbehavior right away and the one who take the report is a 'Pulling Manager.'"

The pulling manager is the one who is responsible for writing the report and take care of the whole case. Tanita William said, "The student who is being pulled from school, because of bad behavior will transfer to the 'Hug Camp'"

The Hug Camp is place where misbehaving students go. It is a special place for care that is different from the usual places. It's a place to show love and care, unless the child has committed a real criminal act. Then it's off to the Court. Other than that, it is a "Hug Camp" where those kids are taken care of. She found out that a lot of kids just wanted a good hug every morning and then everything would be all right. Some of them feel alienated from their families. They feel they are not wanted where they live. They feel isolated. They just need a hug and show of love. They need show of a feeling that they belong to where they live. Some of them may need simple things like a few dollars to buy candy or a soda. Their families are too poor to give them those dollars. Some just want new sneakers or new clothes, but they are not criminals. They are not that bad. They just need little care, a good hug, a show of love. Tanita William says, "96% of those cases can be solved right here at the 'Hug Camp' without ever being reported to the police or court."

Just like Jasper who is 15 and every day at school, he is very mean with his friends and always angry and every other day he fights with his classmates for no reason. Sometimes the students report Jasper to the Pulling Manager, who right away transfers him to the Hug Camp for a month. Because Jasper was fighting his classmate over a candy bar that cost two dollars, and punched him in a face in hug camp, Tanita William said, "The psychiatrist will try to know why he acts like that. She found out Jasper lives with his mom in one bedroom apartment and his mom has a boyfriend who always drinks and likes to fight his mom whenever he comes to her apartment. Whenever Jasper wants to help his mom, she always stops him, saying, 'He is my boyfriend and I love him. This is my apartment and I am paying the rent. When you have your own apartment, then do whatever you want to do."

Jasper tells the psychiatrist, "When I come to school, I am very upset, very mad. I can't do anything to my mom because I really love her. She loves her boyfriend. But in school whenever any student gives me a look I don't like. I just jump on them. I am really angry with my life. I am not happy. I don't know what to do. I really need help. I am in need now! When her boyfriend comes on the weekend to stay with her, I have to leave the apartment and sleep in my neighbor's apartment!"

Jasper in the hug camp shows he is very nice kid. Staying with his mom and her boyfriend is his problem. If we change the environment where he lives, his life will change for good. So they contacted his grandma who lived in a living assistance place by herself. She was happy to have Jasper move and stay with her. That was the turning point in Jasper's life. He completely changed into the most friendly person in school, the most creative person in living assistance. When he stayed with his grandma and saw how the residents in living assistance lived, how lonely they were, he created a nice program called "Weekends with Grandparents." He told his friends in school that living with his grandma was fun, that grandmothers can teach you the family history and still they can tell you bed stories. Besides they really need some help with shopping, cleaning their apartments or laundry or just companions like going to dinner with them, or watching movies. And grandparents are generous too. They give some cash to the one who helps them.

The kids in school like Jasper's idea. They flood to their grandparents who live in assistance on the weekends like shooting stars. The found out Jasper was right, they get bed stories again, help their grandparents, get some cash for when they go back home.

The assisted living on weekends become like amusement parks. Not grandkids alone; they bring their parents too. It's like small family reunions every weekend. The elderly residents don't feel lonely any more. They've started waiting the weekend with hope and love!

The Hug Camp works very well because that good hug and caring in the camp removes any negative thoughts about life. Cool them down, take all the stress out, clean out all stupid ideas in their minds about killing themselves or killing others, put the hope and peace and security in their minds, and you give them new ideas on how to face life with love and feel brave and strong.

Umbilical Cord Apartment

The fourth program is for parents when they get old. Most people when their parents get old, the first thing in their mind is a nursing home. But Professor Tanita William has a better idea called "Umbilical Cord Apartment." This brilliant idea is to move the parents close to their children and children close to their parents through two apartments attached to each other and connected with middle door between the two, like a hotel door. Each apartment has its own entrance, own kitchen, restroom. The middle door between two apartments is like the umbilical cord which used to be the life line between a mother and her child, because when parents get old want that life line again, to get the emotional support and physical support.

So, putting them in the nursing home, leaving them there alone, letting the strangers help them and leaving them in a dark room alone by themselves, waiting for death in this critical age, that is not fair. That is not a happy end for our parents who did everything to grow us up and make us happy. That is a nightmare and inhumane and a big shame.

So, Professor William wants to change the name of nursing homes to "Emergency Homes." She has a point. Emergency homes should be for those who need medical attention every day and those who don't have families or anyone to take care of them and that is an emergency! That makes sense. , Children should care of elderly parents and take on this responsibility with love and be very kind to their parents at this age because they really need to be with their family and children. That a natural feeling and we can't deny it!

Professor William says, " Umbilical Cord Apartments' are a way for you to pay back to your parents and respect the life cycle which is natural. There's nothing wrong with being old. Nothing wrong with our old parents staying among us. It is a blessing to take care of your parents when they get old. It teaches us the meaning of love and life. People should open their mind to know that parents are everything.

Tanita William says, "Mr. Scott Garcia whose parents both died at the nursing home is very sad about that. He always told his wife, Linda, 'That is a big mistake in my life. I don't know why I didn't take care of my parents, why I put them in the nursing home. They were not so ill. We are family of seven. Our parents worked hard to take care of us and raise us without any help from outside. But when we grew up, we just didn't care about them, just like that. That is not fair. I will never forgive myself.' ".

Mr. Scott one day told his wife, Linda, about "Umbilical Cord Apartments," because Linda's mom was still in a nursing home. He explained, "It is simple idea. It is two separate apartments with two private entrances, but both apartments attached to each other. They are connected in the middle with a door that connected them like the umbilical cord which connects the mother with her baby. That is why call umbilical cord apartment. So, my sweetheart, let's move to an umbilical cord apartment and bring your mom from the nursing home. You know nursing home is not cheap. The umbilical cord apartment will be cheaper and save money for us and for your mom too, and still your mom will have her own entrance and own private kitchen, restroom, so both of us will still have privacy."

When we go to work, we can hire somebody for a few hours to look after her. Besides our kids can take care of their grandma when they come back from the school. That will be good for the kids to develop a sense of sharing their time for good cause, taking care of their own grandma."

Linda Scott listened to her husband and they moved to an umbilical cord apartment. Linda said, "When my mom come to stay with me, become my neighbor in the umbilical cord apartment, my mom face shining every day. She become full of life. When she enter my apartment she didn't even use her walker. She walk nicely and happily. My kids were staying with her all the time. They went with her shopping, they cleaned her apartment, My kids changed for real. They became wiser than before my mom came to stay with us. They stopped spending their time on TV or the Internet. They spent their time with their grandma living next-door in her beautiful umbilical cord apartment."

Linda continued, "When my mom became my neighbor in this umbilical cord apartment, I felt reborn. I had a new feeling come to me for the first time in my life. It was a mix of sweetness and astonishment and love and peace. I feel that is the best thing I've done in my life."

Tanita William said, "Parents are everything in our lives. They are the reason we are here. We should never think of leaving them alone when they grow old and looking for the strangers to help them when we can help them ourselves. We should be like Mr. Robert Ray."

Mr. Robert Ray said in his story, "When I dropped off my mom in the nursing home from my house, I remembered my birthdays from the early years of my life. I remember how my mom hugged me, kissed me, gave me all kinds of gifts, , even till I reached 55. I couldn't pay my house mortgage. My mom let me stay with her in her house. Now my mom is 75. I took her to a nursing home from her house. It was not my house. My mom was not sick. She just talked too much to my wife about cleaning the house. My mom is very clean person, my wife not, which is why she convinced me to take her to nursing home for a week, just to feel some change, get some health care.

My mom loves me. That is why she went with me. My wife's plan was to keep my mom in a nursing home for good. I don't know why I obeyed my wife. I remember when I entered the nursing home with my mom she said, with her eyes full of tears, 'Why do you want to leave me here? What did I do to you to keep me here?' She keep saying, 'why, why?'"

All these thoughts come to Robert Ray as soon as he left the nursing home and drove back home. Suddenly Robert Ray said, "I decided to bring my mom home. That was not fair. I did a big U turn on the road. I am glad I hit nobody. I drove back to the nursing home. I noticed a police car behind me. I increased my speed. I didn't stop. I reached the nursing home parking lot. I ran to the front desk, asked about my mom. They told me, 'Just now, they took her to the hospital in an ambulance.' I was shocked. I almost fell down. When the police officer who was chasing me witnessed the conversation, he kept me from falling down, and said, 'Let's go to the hospital, you don't have to drive. I am taking you in the police car. I hope your mom is okay.'

He hold my hand, gave me a hug, and we both ran to the police car. We reached the hospital very soon. I went into intensive care room. I saw my mom on a bed. When she saw me she said, 'I knew you were going to come back. You're my son, my baby boy.'

"I cried. I said, "Forgive me, Mom, I will never do it again.""

My mom said, "Do you remember when you were at high school? I told you the mistakes we make in our life is like a compass. It redirects us in the right direction. When we get lost in life, then we come back to the right direction to complete the game of life safely, peacefully. I forgive you, my son. Take me home. I want to be in my own bed. Listen, on the way home, can you stop at McDonalds? I want a cup of senior coffee, to feel fresh!!"

Robert Ray continued, "The doctor came to discharge my mom. He said, 'She is okay. It was just a panic attack. It happens to most people who come to nursing homes for the first time. It is feeling of fear, lost, uncertainty. To be honest, some people cannot take it. It leads to this panic, sometime to death. I am glad you come very soon. That helped a lot. Please try to take care of your mom. Remember, nothing is wrong with being old!'

"I took my mom home. My mom died at 95 in her own home with me and all her family around. In the 20 years from that incident, I never missed a breakfast or a dinner with my mom. My wife become her best friend.

"The police officer who took me to the hospital became a family friend. I remember he said, 'If you hadn't taken that U turn, I would have given you two tickets. One for moving violation, the second for putting your mom in nursing home while she was okay to live in her own house, but, it was good move. I hope everybody takes that move and cares for their own parents instead of keeping them in a dark room in an unknown nursing home without visiting them till they die alone, because that is not fair.' "

Tanita Williams created a TV channel for seniors called "I Am Here" that the umbilical cord apartments, she created are designed to connect the nursing home population with their families and the world. "I Am Here" played an active role in connecting seniors with their families. Tanita Williams created a beautiful company called the, "Flying Wheelchair Company," which helps those in nursing homes to travel from their rooms in nursing homes to see their families. The company agent will come to the nursing home with their wheelchairs and access cars to take the passengers from their rooms in the nursing home up to the airport, through the security checkpoint up to their seats in the aircraft. And there will be another agent waiting for them when they arrive to their destination to help them the same way till they reach their family's house or apartment. With this amazing service the nursing home population will start traveling safely and comfortably to have Thanksgiving dinner with their families and Christmas too, as well as the graduation ceremonies of their children and grandchildren, family weddings, and birthdays of their grandchildren.

The "I Am Here" TV Channel had an amazing story about Ms. Rosemary Rossvelt who went missing from her family when she was 85. Rosemary, from Houston, Texas, had a short memory and after a few years, her family presumed she was dead. But they saw her on the "I Am Here" TV Channel for seniors. They saw how she ended up in a nursing home, how she was treated, and got her memory back, just like a miracle.

Rosemary said, "I am still alive. I still can make a difference in my life and in the lives of the people around me and my family too." Rosemary's grandson who is a millionaire in Houston, Texas, brought his grandma in his private jet from the nursing home in Albany, New York and called his grandma "the forgotten queen," bringing her to live with him on his ranch in Houston. And now that she lives with him on his ranch, he treats her like a real queen! She moved from an unknown nursing home in Albany, New York to a beautiful ranch in Houston, Texas with her grandson. That's a tribute to the "I Am Here" TV Channel.

It Happens House

The fifth program, called "It Happens House," is for the homeless. Professor William said, "Anybody can be homeless. Whatever we have in our hand, we can lose. That is a law of life, just like anybody can die just like that. Accidents happen. It's the nature of human life on this planet earth. If you don't have a paycheck for four weeks or two weeks, you are homeless. If you file for bankruptcy, you are homeless. If you don't pay your house mortgage, you are homeless. If your apartment or house is in a fire you are homeless. If there is flooding or a hurricane, you are homeless. Homelessness is a big issue in our daily life. We should face it with courage and wisdom. So, Tanita William said, "It Happens House" should be a permanent place for every citizen who had trouble or problems or had hardships to find a place to live. It should be a place to save human dignity and human safety and should be very safe and comfortable for anyone who lives there and everybody in the country should share in building it, because anybody can be in this situation. It should be a great sign of how we take care of our citizens when they are still alive and they want somebody to bail them out. Just as pyramids are a sign of ancient Egyptian civilization, this should be a sign of life in the 21st Century!!!

The last program for Professor Tanita William was for Inmates. In this program, Tanita William said, "I want to change the classical view of inmates who come out from prison broke and have no clothes and sometimes no place to go, changing from tearful faces, to cheerful faces, to people with big smiles, hope and peace."

Because, Tanita William said, "The number of inmates and people on probation are close to five million. That is a big number. Just like the population of Norway, which is one of the richest country in the world. The program is called 'Hope from Inside.'"

This program is designed to give the inmates hope and a real second chance for a better life, to accept those who committed a crime and served their time to join the real world again, to become good citizens again.

The program starts with simple basic things.

First , when inmates finish their time and come out of prison, they should have full freedom. That means no probation time and no parole officer to report to.

Eliminate the question in the job application, "Have you ever done time in prison or been convicted of any crime or felony?"

Tanita William wants to keep the private part of inmates' lives open only to prison management and courts and police, not to the public unless they commit a crime the public should know about.

When inmates finish their time, leave those people alone. If they commit any crime again, they should go to prison again, but this question or job applications makes it hard for inmates to get jobs and at the same time gives the inmates feelings of inferiority and discriminates them from the rest of society. Nobody is perfect. So, we should give them a real second chance to move forward and become good citizens again.

Tanita William says, "Hope from Inside starts with a one year special program for learning three subjects, which are geography, history, and science and technology."

Those three subjects will clean the brain and minds of inmates from the dust of prison time and a criminal mentality and the sad environment they were living in and open doors to the whole world of hope. They will know the real world and how many countries in the world, how many people in the world, the ecosystem and weather so they can have a new outlook on everything around them and discover the beauty of the world, and then discover the beauty inside them. History will show them the human culture and human races and tribes and human identity.

When did humans first dwell on the earth? They will learn human civilization and culture, the diversity of human colors and thinking and behavior through human history. This will develop a better understanding of human beings, of life itself. This will open inmates minds wider and wider and move them from a criminal circle which is full of hatred and revenge and stupidity, to wise thinking and touching the opportunities in life through the history of human life.

The third subject should teach them science and technology, because science will teach them the solid truth about life and gravitation, physics, mathematics, with a little concentration on basic human physiology and human anatomy and human embryology and basic human health. Science will remind the inmates about the origin of life and how life is amazing and organized and beautiful and interesting. If you look at life from the door of science, every day you find something interesting to explore always, something new take the focus and attention off inmates and to a new world of adventure and fun. Encourage them to spend their time in this new area.

Technology can liberate inmates' imaginations from any obstacles that stop them from soaring high in their lives just like eagles and birds and gain the ultimate meaning of freedom. They can taste the new nectar of life they have never dreamed of, move freely with their lives in safe and better places, build real hope about their future.

The second part of hope from inside is to work for one year, 12 months, seven days a week, at a full time job for 8 hours a day. Morning shift starts at 6 a.m. to 2:30 p.m. and two days from 6 a.m. to 10 a.m. four hours on Sundays and Saturdays. Each inmate gets a job according to the field in which he or she has experience. This job should be in collaboration with companies who have contracts to pay the inmates their whole salary at the end of the 12 months, so they can get all their money when they come out to start a new life, so they will not come out broke.

Tanita William said, "This program of two years, one year for learning life skills through knowledge of geography and history and science and technology and one year working for 7 days a week will give them real hope, because working for 7 days a week will bring inmates to the normal life of normal people. Wake up, take a shower, take your breakfast, go to your job, and earn money to help yourself and your family and pay taxes to help your country and the needy people, to be a good citizen."

After finishing the two years of program, the rewards will be:

1. No probation

2. No parole officer to report to

3. Get your driver's license back

4. Free bank account to put your money in

5. Most inmates when they come out will have problems finding a place for themselves because of their credit. So, Professor Tanita William has a beautiful idea called "Co-Signer Manager." The Co-Signer Manager is a person who co-signs rental agreements for inmates when they come out. The co- signer will work with inmates for four years till they get themselves together.

6. Affordable medical insurance for inmates for four years

7. Right to vote like any citizen

8. Right to travel outside the country like any citizen with no restrictions

Professor William said, "With the two year program which should be the last two years of inmates' time in prison, the inmate will have a real hope to start new life full of confidence. Because they will come out with big money in their account, with medical insurance and a co-signer to help them to find a place to live, and, most important, they come back with their freedom again - no probation, no parole officer, just free like anybody else. When they want to apply for new job, they will find job, thanks to applications without the conviction question. Just hit the road, Jack!"

Tanita William continued, "Dwight Jackson ended up in the 'Hope from Inside Program.' As soon as he completed his time, he went to the airport and traveled to Costa Rica to meet his 'x' girlfriend who had a restaurant on the beach. When he reached her there, his girlfriend said to him, 'I guess everybody who knew you will think you died in prison after 12 years, but now you are here on a beach with money and a different mindset. Now you want to marry me. You never thought of marriage in your life. You always said you were a playboy only. You have changed for real."

Tanita William said, "The program is good and is real and it works with 100% of the inmates who took the program. Because it really gives them a second chance and makes them feel they can do it, . they really do it."

Tanita William ended her article by saying, "The 21st Century is the human century where human health and food and water and education should be available to anybody on earth. Humans should be very kind to their pets, especially to dogs, because the dog is man's best friend and does a lot for human beings. She appealed to all human beings to stop removing or cutting the tails of dogs, because the tails help dogs with their balance.

All those thoughts came to John Patrick while he was in his favorite spot at night on New Haven Green and after his friend Martin Franklin left him.

He was mindful of a lot of things, but had one feeling after talking to Martin Franklin. *I want to change my life, to be a better person, and I don't want to go back to Jessica.* And then he fell asleep on the grass on his favorite spot on New Haven Green!!! Just like that!!!

Chapter 7

Early in the morning on New Haven Green John Patrick woke up, jumping from the ground saying, "Please don't kill me. I am not a criminal. I am a human being. What is wrong with you? I left the house for you. I am happy with my life, with my smell. I don't harm nobody. I am free to choose my way of life. I hate prejudice. I am regular man. I am a pigeon man. Ask the pigeons in the Green. Every morning I feed them. I talk to them. They are my friends. They too nice. Pigeons harm nobody. They are beautiful animals."

Jessica was the one who woke John Patrick that morning, but this time she had a gun in her hand. She said, "Stop it. Go and get a job. I just came to remind you I am not playing. Stop saying 'I am a pigeon man.'"

John Patrick interrupted her saying, "Why? Pigeons are symbols of peace. Why do people like Spiderman?

Spiders are poisonous. I am myself. Leave me alone, please"

Jessica left the Green very soon and hid her gun.

John Patrick was really upset for a moment, and suddenly started laughing. He become very happy. He said to himself, "I know now I am in the right direction. I feel somebody is really jealous of my life. Jessica is not happy with her life. She wants to become a killer. That's her choice because the money makes her blind. She can't see anything in life but money. It is very sad, but I am going to hit the road and get a deluxe breakfast. I didn't eat dinner last night because I was upset, but now I am very happy.

"I remember last night my buddy, Martin, put some money in my hand. Let's see how much he put in. It is a 10 dollar bill. Wow, I am rich. I am going to get my breakfast now and see what is going on after that, but I promise myself from today I am going to be a new person. No more Jessica in my life. I will never go back to her again."

After John Patrick had his breakfast from McDonalds, he headed back to New Haven Green. When he reached the Green, he found all the homeless sitting together in circle. Jack Nelson stood in middle talking. When he arrived at the gathering, Jack Nelson stopped talking.

John Patrick said, "It looks your guys have a meeting." Jack Nelson said, "Yes, my friend. It is about you. Ms. Jefferson saw Jessica early this morning come to the Green with gun. My friend, listen to me carefully. We don't have time, you must leave Connecticut very soon, now, you and me. We are going to the Greyhound bus station to book a ticket for tomorrow to my uncle in Santa Fe, New Mexico. Tonight you are going to sleep in the shelter in Fairhaven, because in the shelter Jessica can't come over there with any weapon. On the way to Greyhound we are going to stop at Goodwill to buy you some clothes and shoes and bags to carry your stuff and then one more stop at barber shop to get a haircut and shave your beard. Let's go now and don't say anything. Please my friend, we don't have any time. Tonight everybody will come to the shelter to say goodbye!!! This is very serious. We must act quickly now! I already called my uncle in Santa Fe, New Mexico. As soon as you arrive at the bus station, one of his employees will be waiting for you and take you to the farm."

John Patrick was very calm, just like Jack Nelson. They went straight ahead to the shelter to spend the rest of the day and the night. At 6 a.m. next day, Jack Nelson and John Patrick took a taxi to New Haven's Union Station so John Patrick could catch the 7 a.m. Greyhound bus to Santa Fe, New Mexico.

In the taxi, John Patrick was crying, saying, "I want to see my kids before I go."

Jack Nelson said to him, "Listen to me. I promise you I will bring your kids to you in New Mexico. I know it is very hard, but you must leave now, very soon. It looks like this crazy lady is following you. Just calm down my friend. Your life comes first."

John Patrick stop crying. "I agree with you my friend." The taxi reached New Haven's Union Station. Jack Nelson said, "I will get you a cup of coffee and some doughnuts. Just wait for me here." Jack Nelson brought the coffee and doughnuts, give John Patrick a good hug, and said, "I promise I will find a legal way to bring your kids to your custody. Just promise me to stop drinking alcohol, keep a job, and try to find your own place, so I can build a strong case for you in court. Take care of yourself, my friend."

John Patrick had small back bag. With a coffee in his hand he went to the Greyhound bus stand. Before John Patrick reached the bus where the bus driver was boarding passengers checking their tickets, John Patrick heard somebody call his name. He knew the voice very well. He turned to make sure.

It was Jessica. She said, "Stop, Mr. Coward. I am going to kill you now."

John Patrick turned so quickly the coffee in his hand spilled on the floor. He fell down. Jessica fired at him, but when John Patrick fell, the bullet hit the Greyhound bus driver in the head. The police were right there at the spot where the shooting started. Even Jack Nelson hadn't left the station. He was waiting far away to make sure his friend boarded safely. He saw what had happened.

Jessica was about to fire more times, but the police were right there. They shot her right away in the head. She fell down. John Patrick, already on the ground, saw Jessica fall and started crying. By that time, Jack Nelson ran and stopped him from running to Jessica. Jack Nelson told the police, "He is my brother. He just saw the blood and panicked, He doesn't need any medical attention. I am taking him home now.

Jack Nelson took John Patrick away from the Union Station, comforting him saying to him, "Jessica is dead. The police killed her. It is very sad but that's what happens. Listen, it is very hard, but is over. Now you have two kids waiting for you. Their mom just passed away. They lost their mom for good so they need you now. You don't have to travel now. Now you have to go to your kids. You can't do anything about what happened. I will be with you to the end because you are my friend. You are a good man. Everybody in New Haven Green will be with you."

After a while, John Patrick calmed. "You are right, my friend. My kids need me now more than any time before. I am not going to let them down. But I promise you I will never give up again. I am going to live my life the way I want. I will drink the best drink on the earth, which is water and milk. I am not going to stop breathing fresh air. I am going to travel to the best places in the earth which are mountains, seas and oceans. I am going to enjoy every moment of my life with my kids. I will never let my kids down. I will never let anybody make me do things his way, because now I know my way!"

About the Author

Abdelgaffer Elyamani is a Sudanese American born in the city of Omdurman in Sudan. Graduate from the University of Madras in India with a bachelor of Science Major Zoology. Currently working as a passenger assistance to help people with disabilities to travel in Denver International Airport for more than 15 years in a row.

Special thanks to the Hampden Press team, 9955 E. Hampden Ave., Denver, CO 80231, for corrections and printing my first book.

www.ingramcontent.com/pod-product-compliance
Lightning Source LLC
Chambersburg PA
CBHW071127130626
46556CB00012B/3117